WITHDRAWN

CUENTO
DE LUZ

To Jèssica, our little girl of the forest: thank you for embracing us.
Mom and Dad love you.

— Nívola Uyá y Marc Ayats —

This book is printed on **Stone Paper** with silver **Cradle to Cradle™** certification.

Cradle to Cradle™ is one of the most demanding ecological certification systems, awarded to products that have been conceived and designed in an ecologically intelligent way.

Cradle to Cradle™ recognizes that environmentally safe materials are used in the manufacturing of Stone Paper which have been designed for re-use after recycling. The use of less energy in a more efficient way, together with the fact that no water, trees nor bleach are required, were decisive factors in awarding this valuable certification.

Bathing in the Forest
Text © 2019 Nívola Uyá y Marc Ayats
Illustrations © 2019 Nívola Uyá
This edition © 2019 Cuento de Luz SL
Calle Claveles, 10 | Urb. Monteclaro | Pozuelo de Alarcón | 28223 | Madrid | Spain
www.cuentodeluz.com
Original title in Spanish: *Un baño de bosque*
English translation by Jon Brokenbrow
Printed in PRC by Shanghai Chenxi Printing Co., Ltd. August 2019, print number 1695-9
ISBN: 978-84-16733-58-3

Nívola Uyá ✳ Marc Ayats

BATHING
IN THE
FOREST

I am the little girl of the
forest.

I dive between
the roots and leaves,
and take care of this place.

Submerged deep in the shadows
of the trees, I watch the people
who walk through my home.

I welcome them all with
a loving embrace.

From the top of the tallest oak,
I can feel the footsteps of
Mr. Grayshadow.

He is walking slowly,
in no particular direction.
He is full of loneliness;
he feels empty,
as if something were missing from his life.

Mr. Grayshadow needs to bathe in the forest.

Near the stream, I can see Mrs. Graystone.
She is frightened, and her legs are shaking.
It is as if a great weight were bearing down upon her soul.

I take her by the hand, and offer her a bath in the forest.

Sitting next to the fox's den, I can hear the footsteps of a little boy drawing near. It's the youngest of the Graystone family. He keeps looking around nervously.

"What's the matter?" I ask him.

"Every time I take a path, it leads nowhere," he replies, biting his lip.

I walk over to him, and I whisper:

"Don't worry.
Come here and bathe in the forest."

If you're ever feeling gray . . .

Relax for a moment, close your eyes, and breathe in the ancient aromas of the earth.

Enjoy the intense flavor of the wild berries.

Watch as the sunlight filters through the leaves, dappling the beautiful shapes and colors of the woodland flowers.

Listen to the secret messages of the birds, and the graceful dance of the branches in the wind.